D0471258

© 1992 Jim Henson Productions, Inc. MUPPET PRESS, MUPPETS, MUPPET KIDS, and character names and likenesses are trademarks of Jim Henson Productions, Inc. All rights reserved, including the right to reproduce this book or portions thereof in any form. VALUES TO GROW ON is a trademark of Grolier Inc.
Published by Grolier Direct Marketing, Danbury, Connecticut

Printed in the U.S.A.

ISBN 0-7172-8269-4

JIM HENSON'S MUPPETS
IN

What's Fair Is Fair

A Book About Sharing

By Louise Gikow • Illustrated by Tom Leigh

GROLIER

It was a beautiful summer morning, and the county fair had just come to town. The tents and rides were set up in the big field behind the school. In a few moments, the fair would be open for business.

Piggy and Kermit stared at the poster by the ticket booth. RAFFLE! it proclaimed. ONLY TWENTY-FIVE CENTS. THE WINNER WILL RIDE AT THE HEAD OF THE BIG PARADE!

"Couldn't you just see me riding at the head of the parade?" Piggy asked Kermit. "I really want to win that raffle!"

"So do I," Kermit said.

The ticket booth opened for business at nine o'clock sharp. Soon Piggy and Kermit were at the head of the line.

Piggy reached into her pocket for her money. She had emptied out her piggy bank earlier that morning and had brought every cent she had for the fair and raffle tickets.

But her money wasn't there.

Piggy tried another pocket and another. But all her pockets were empty.

"What's the matter?" Kermit asked.

"My money!" Piggy gasped. "It must have fallen out of my pocket. It's all gone!"

"What am I going to do?" moaned Piggy. "I saved up for months to come to the fair."

"What about your mom?" Kermit asked. "Could you run home and ask her to help? I'm sure she'd understand."

"No," Piggy said. "She's really busy, and I don't want to bother her. Besides," Piggy added, sighing, "she's always telling me to be more careful. She'd probably say 'I told you so.'"

"Look," Kermit said. "Don't worry. I bought plenty of tickets. You can share mine. And here's a quarter for the raffle."

"Are you sure?" Piggy said, brightening.

"I'm sure," said Kermit.

"Oh, Kermie! You're the best pal ever!" said Piggy. "I'll pay you back . . . I promise!"

First Piggy dragged Kermit off to the food stands.

"Mmm...look!" she said. "Candy apples... my favorite. Could we have one, Kermie? Please?"

"Sure, Piggy," Kermit said, buying her one.

Then ... "Oh!" Piggy said, crossing over to an arcade game. "What a cute little teddy bear! Could we play, Kermie?"

"Uh, sure, Piggy," said Kermit, giving her three tickets.

Piggy wanted to see the Hall of Mirrors ... so
that's where they went next.

And she wanted to see the prizewinning
rabbits, too....

Finally she wanted to go on the Ferris wheel.

At the end of the day, Piggy and Kermit stood in the crowd, waiting for the raffle drawing. They held their tickets tightly and crossed their fingers. They both wanted to win.

Mayor Muller pulled the winning number out of a hat.

"The number is..." Mayor Muller paused, looking around the crowd. Piggy's heart jumped as she looked down again. "Thirty-two!" the mayor proclaimed.

Piggy looked at her ticket. She could hardly believe her eyes. She started to jump up and down and wave both her arms.

"I won!" she shouted. "I won!"

Piggy raced up to the platform with her ticket. The mayor congratulated her.

"Looks like you'll be riding at the head of the parade," she said. "You're a lucky little girl."

"I know," Piggy said, beaming. "I am."

Piggy raced over to Kermit. "I won!" she laughed, hopping up and down. "I won! Isn't it wonderful?"

Then Piggy saw Kermit's face. He looked a little sad. And Piggy suddenly realized that while she had won the raffle, Kermit had lost.

Piggy thought about how nice Kermit had been all day. He had shared all his tickets with her—and that meant he could only go on half as many rides and have half as many treats himself. But he had never complained.

I am lucky, Piggy thought. *But not because I won the raffle. I'm lucky because I have a sharing, caring friend like Kermit.*

It didn't take Piggy a long time to figure out a way to thank him.

Piggy walked up to the mayor and tapped her on the shoulder. Then she whispered something in the mayor's ear.

At first she shook her head, but Piggy didn't give up. She whispered something to her again. The mayor stared at her and nodded. Then she shook Piggy's hand.

When Piggy joined Kermit again, she looked
very pleased with herself.

"What was that all about?" Kermit asked
her.

Piggy whispered something in Kermit's ear.
Slowly Kermit began to smile.

"Are you sure?" he asked.

"I'm sure," Piggy replied.

Everyone agreed that the big parade that evening was the grandest ever. Marching at the head of it was a beautiful white horse. And on the horse sat . . . Piggy *and* Kermit, waving to the crowd!

"Isn't it exciting?" whispered Piggy.

"You bet," said Kermit. "Thanks for sharing your prize with me."

"Thank *you*!" Piggy smiled back. "It's easy to share with a sharing friend!"

Let's Talk About Sharing

Kermit and Piggy had a great time riding at the front of the parade. Piggy was really glad she had shared her prize. But sometimes sharing isn't easy…especially when you're asked to share something you really like or want.

Here are some questions about sharing for you to think about:

Have you ever shared something that was important to you? How did it make you feel?

Do you like it when your friends share with you?

Why do you think it's important to share?